INTERVIEW

WITH A

#VANLIFER

M.K. WILLIAMS

Printed in the United States of America

Publisher: MK Williams Publishing, LLC
Library of Congress Control Number: 2022916829
ISBN:
978-1-952084-26-3 (eBook)
978-1-952084-27-0 (Paperback)

Cover Art: Canva Stock Image

Mary K. Williams
https://1mkwilliams.com
1mkwilliamsauthor@gmail.com

Works by M.K. Williams

Fiction
The Project Collusion Series
Nailbiters
Architects

The Feminina Series
The Infinite-Infinite
The Alpha-Nina

Other Fiction
The Games You Cannot Win
Escaping Avila Chase
Enemies of Peace

Non-Fiction
Self-Publishing for the First-Time Author
Book Marketing for the First-Time Author
How to Write Your First Novel: A Guide for Aspiring Fiction Authors
Going Wide: Self-Publishing Your Books Outside The Amazon Ecosystem
Author Your Ambition: The Complete Self-Publishing Workbook for First-Time Authors

Table of Contents

Interview with a #Vanlifer

"I see," I mumble as Ursula shows me the inverter nestled underneath the storage area in the back of the van. No matter how many times I've interviewed full-time nomads, I can't seem to get as excited as they do about their energy setups and water capacity. That's because I've never lived it. I've never relied on the exact wattage and gallons allotted in a finite space. I've never had to think about where the power comes from or where the water is sourced from. Not yet.

Ursula beams with pride at the watt-hour capacity. Digital nomads need a reliable power source to keep their electric burners brewing coffee, and their WiFi hotspots hooked up so they can keep up with their posting schedule. Even after multiple encounters with vanlifers, I still feel like these terms are a foreign language. Inverters. Photovoltaic cells. It's lost on me. And most of the vanlifer groupies too. Most are eager to see the well-designed compact living space and the breathtaking views.

Each year the trend grows with more newbies opting to try their hand at life on the road. The resale market for gently used camper vans is telling of how well it goes. Vanlife is not for the faint of heart. Constant repairs and creative solutions go hand-in-hand with the freedom this lifestyle affords.

The first part of every interview with those who embrace vanlife usually focuses on their home on wheels. But that's not what I'm really here for, and neither are you.

I only arrived at the park an hour before this extensive van tour. With my rental car parked and the sun still descending in the valley, I head out to the trail leading to the base of Yosemite Falls. A flat, paved walk, I give myself a few extra moments to enjoy the park before it was all lost to the darkness of night. The sun hits the water in the most spectacular way, the droplets like diamonds scattering to the wind. Thinking of my interviewees and their unique predicament, I savored that sunset — every blinding facet of it. I didn't linger long. The gloaming is near. I return to my car, determined to be precisely on time.

I rest against the driver's side door, staring at the neighboring van. Just as the sun dipped below the valley, the last bit of orange gone from the sky, the door to the van slides open and two people step out onto the gravel. The sky is a light purple, gradually darkening, imperceptibly marching towards brown into black.

I knew they would be disarmingly beautiful. I had seen their photos online. But I half expected them to look a little worse for the wear, a little rough around the edges. Like we all do in real life. I expected them to be like any other human whose curated social media feed is only beautiful photos, and real life is a ten percent dip at best. No, they look as perfect as ever. Not that looks matter. But then again, yes, they do.

Ursula's strawberry blonde hair is braided into a clean plait. Set against her fleece jacket, she looks like she designed her style to mimic Taylor Swift's *evermore* album cover, although she cultivated her signature look decades before Swift was born.

Peter wears a faded black tee shirt with the signature "climate change bites" logo used by the pair on their blog and social media. The design, a set of fangs about to bite into the earth, looked reminiscent of a '90s grunge rock band logo. Peter's long black hair sticks out at the top; it adds to the look. His hairstyle has been more fluid, changing with the decades, according to a post in August 2021 showing his style evolution. His long locks of the '70s were shorn and buzzed and regrown. The pictures in their camper tell the story of so many lives lived in their years, different eras and styles, but the two of them never change.

Yes, my interview was with Peter and Ursula. *The* Peter and Ursula. The couple behind the popular #Vamplife account. While the pair is part of the drool-worthy and enviable vanlife community, posting their life from the road on Instagram, they are also part of a much more secretive community: vampires.

Of all the interviews I've conducted with digital nomads, #vanlifers, wanderers, and the like, this one has to be my most unique. Usually, I get a pitch from an up-and-coming influencer or couple with a new spin on the creator economy. They live on a boat instead of in a van. They only work with sustainable brands. They have a new course available to help office workers leave their cubicles and pursue small-scale entrepreneurship. Something that they think sounds unique but has actually been done already.

The world has changed. With millennials and Gen Z leading the charge into the new economy of influence and online content, people understand the power of P.R. and the value of a good interview to expand their platform. Which means I get lots of pitches.

But Peter and Ursula were elusive. For the first time in a long time, I had to be the one to reach out to them. Again, and again, and again. Finally, they agreed to an interview to set the record straight on their life, experiences, political stance, and how they handle their newfound level of internet celebrity.

But first, we needed the weather to cooperate. While they're comfortable sitting together in their van during the day to avoid the sun, Peter and Ursula need cloud cover to move from campsite to campsite. The thunderstorms two days ago were the perfect cover for them to leave their property and meet me here. As droughts continue to plague the west coast, they have been able to visit public campsites less and less — a new complication to their already difficult lives.

We agreed to meet in a public space, with lots of other campers around. The pair have been perfectly amiable and seem just like your friendly hipsters next door on their social media, but I have to say I was relieved by this suggestion. Surely, two vampires wouldn't attack a reporter at a National Park with dozens of potential witnesses nearby.

And my fear of the couple isn't unique. Since Bram Stoker first exposed their kind to the world in 1897, humans have had an understandable fear and unhealthy obsession with vampires.

While Ursula is fastening the bungee cords keeping their storage bins in place after showing off their unique system, the other campers open and close their van doors and start their own fires for the night.

"Fans?" I ask as Peter clocks some of the onlookers, those who keep looking at us instead of focusing on their kindling.

"Maybe. Not everyone knows who we are. It is nice to meet people who've never heard of us. But we have more and more run-ins with followers, which is nice. It gives us the energy to keep posting and creating. But every so often, we meet with the other kind. The not-so-nice kind." Peter leaves the implication there, dangling so obviously in front of me.

"We know who we are, and we have people who love and support us, and that is what matters. It's important to have a thick skin when you are sharing your whole life, your whole person, online. We have decades of practice in that department," Ursula adds as she flips her blonde braid over her shoulder.

"Yeah, we're used to the comments and stares. It's part of the territory," Peter says as he adds a starter brick to the metal tin and lights a fire. The pair have staked claim to a picnic area with a bench, a rusted fire pit, and just enough flat space to pop up a few camp chairs and a tripod for their camera. Peter angles it towards the opening in the trees, a perfect window to the sky. They'll use our interview time for the real work — photography. Ursula's long-exposure images of the Milky Way over National Parks have been a fan favorite for years.

Next, Ursula shows me the cab of the van as the first stars begin to appear in the night sky. She pulls out their toolbox and backup gear stored in large plastic bins. "We don't have to access these often, which is great." Then she guides me to the side so we can access the interior through the sliding van door. As Ursula opens the side door, I see the familiar white and cream walls that grace their Instagram feed. Contrary to popular fiction, the pair do not sleep in a coffin. "We stay couped up in here for 12 to 14 hours at a time, depending on the time of year, so we wanted this space to be a welcome oasis."

The couple has a unique setup. The front of the van is completely blocked off from the living space. "We can't risk window shades falling or slipping even a little bit during the day. We learned from our mistakes early. It was easier to wall it off. It makes the cab feel a little cramped when we are driving, but we tend to stay in one place for several days or sometimes weeks, so we've optimized for living, not driving."

The interior is cozy and well-lived. I can tell they didn't hide everything before my arrival. A book lies open on their cushioned bench positioned against the wall that divides the cab from the living space. Postcard-sized posters of popular vampire movies, shows, and books hang on the wall. The pair have an acute sense of humor.

"We opted to remove our kitchen completely. At first, we wanted to have the option to resell, and a single burner stove and sink would be much better for potential buyers. But it took up so much space, and we never used it. We kept thinking, 'oh, when we have friends visit, we'll want to be able to entertain them.' But you're our first guest in almost a decade. We took out the kitchen area and added these two movable benches, so we have another sitting area separate from our bed. We still have the outdoor shower hook up, so if we get muddy on a hike we can spray off before going inside. That's the most water we usually need. We have one small refrigerator here, but it takes up hardly any room, so we kept it."

I nod along, agreeing with the logic. "Oh, don't worry. We have a pot to boil some water and picked up some instant coffee powder for you." As she says this, I hear Peter approaching. He comes up behind me and reaches for one of the movable benches, unlatching it to reveal a storage container within. He grabs the items Ursula mentioned and heads back to the campfire.

I thank him as Ursula continues the tour, but he is already out of earshot. Perhaps.

"Come on in." She beckons me to step up into the van.

As I look around, a few things catch my eye. This van doesn't feel nearly as cramped compared to other vans converted to living spaces. While other van lifers try to maximize square footage between storage and sleeping, Peter and Ursula don't have that challenge. Their bed setup still takes up a considerable amount of space. Ironic, given that they don't have to sleep.

"We thought about removing the bed completely a few years back. About the same time, we realized that the one thing we really needed that we weren't getting was quiet time. Time for our brains to just stop. We kept the bed and started a meditation practice. We started with five minutes, then ten, then twenty. Now we have worked up to a three-hour meditation practice each day. It gives us time to process this lifetime of brain matter, all these thoughts."

The pair have the luxury of that time. Trapped inside while the sun is up, they can meditate and still run their multiple online businesses all day before escaping to the great outdoors each evening. "It turns out that decades of not sleeping is bad for you, even if you're a vampire. We've done our best work since we started slowing down and taking the time to think. Like, really think."

Ursula doesn't have to point out the next element to me. It is obvious immediately. There are no windows. "We have a double layer surrounding the entire living space, so there are no potential seams where daylight could leak in. We also have a security setup with video to see if anyone is trying to breach the van during the day. In addition to our sponsor SuperSecure, which we advertise, we have some redundancies. We trust SuperSecure, but if people know the system, they could try to hack it, and we need to have a backup. We can't risk these doors opening in the daylight or someone hotwiring the cab and driving away with us in the back." The challenges of being internet famous rear their head once more.

As I take a final look around their sparse interior, I catch a few small tchotchkes. A chihuahua bobblehead wearing a sarape and sombrero on their nightstand. A tiny moose figurine on a shelf. Souvenirs from their life on the road, tokens from a previous decade. To look at their home, it looks normal, just like any other vanlife setup — picture-worthy, minimalist, clean.

I duck back out of the van and Ursula locks it. We approach the fire and Peter hands me the coffee as Ursula settles into her camp chair. The fire between us is bright and warm. I can see the other fires around us, campers roasting hot dogs or marshmallows, enjoying their dinner before turning in. Darkness has settled in for the evening, and so have we. The three of us won't be turning in. We have a lot of ground to cover in one night.

"So, what do you want to know?" Peter offers.

With that opening, I dive into my questions. "How did this all start?" I let them decide what I'm referring to. Their online presence, their vampire life, or their penchant for living in a van.

They elect the final option.

"Well, we had a little bit of money saved up and we knew we needed a break from the city," Ursula starts.

San Francisco in the 1970s is different from today in many ways. But it is also the same. With the proximity to Muir Woods National Monument, the pair elected to make it a weekend habit to retreat to the woods. To commune with nature. To escape into the trees.

"Even when the weather was San Francisco summer cold, we would go. We'd pack up first thing after work on Fridays and regretfully drive back on Sunday evenings. We had started to talk about longer trips and made a plan to do a summer-long sabbatical." Ursula looks at Peter at this point, waiting for some unspoken signal. Whatever it was, I didn't catch it.

With a sigh, Ursula continues. "We decided to take

Memorial Day weekend to go to Yosemite. We knew it would be crowded, but we wanted to do a longer trip in the van to see if we would actually like it. We elected to stay at Mariposa Grove among the beautiful towering trees. We figured it would be a little less busy than this part of the park," she gestures to the darkness around us with her hand.

"That's when it happened." Peter cut in abruptly. His voice contains hints of anger, the menacing call that so many have written about, the predatory purr of a vampire.

The pair sit silently for a moment, reverent. I realize what they are referring to. *"That's when it happened."* As in, when they became vampires. They both stare ahead at the fire between us as if they are watching a replay of this moment on an invisible screen.

I shift in my camp chair, and the canvas supporting me feels flimsy. Not up to the task of keeping me and the weight of what I've just learned from falling to the ground. The conversations from other campers, their fires in the periphery, filter through the trees, their chatter incongruent with this significant revelation. Of all the places for us to meet, to go back to this park. An entirely different section but very close to the scene of the crime.

"We don't go to Mariposa Grove anymore." Ursula's

voice is so small and quiet that I can barely hear it. This is not what I expected. I didn't think they would share this with me, this soon. I'm thrown off balance; I'm out of my depth in this interview. I usually talk to people about their bucket list trips and social media growth metrics. This is too personal, too traumatic.

I clear my throat, buying another moment. "I would expect not," my pathetic answer. I might have guessed it. Their previous posts on social media seem to indicate a special connection to Yosemite. A kinship, a complicated familial relationship. They've never talked about their transformation before, not on any of their channels. Based on their comments this evening, I now know they were born into their vampiric life in Yosemite.

Fitting, as the origin of the park's name is from the Miwok tribe who originally lived in the valley before the Mariposa Battalion forced them off of their land. The word means "one who kills." Perhaps the Miwok had an encounter with the vampire who infected Peter and Ursula. But this is just speculation on my part.

"Our maker was little help," Ursula adds, her tone changing as she refocuses the conversation. "He was as old as the trees in Mariposa Grove, barely lucid. We had to figure most of this out on our own. Some we knew from legends, but there is so much more that they don't even touch."

"It shifted our plans pretty quickly," Peter continues with a sharpness to his words that hadn't been there before. The intensity reminds me that he is more than human, more than my weak frame could ever be. "Our 'sabbatical' from work started then and there. The virus was very painful and we took months to recover, although no one ever fully recovers from it," he gestures to his body as he says this.

This has been proven scientifically. Dr. Anders Rice, out of Germany, has been researching and publishing his findings on vampires and the vampiric germ. And with good reason. Dr. Rice was infected two centuries ago. The inspiration for at least one fictional vampire M.D., this vamp doc has focused his efforts on helping his own kind. In his Nobel-winning research from 2018, he asserted that the vampiric virus works much like HIV. Many are familiar with the mechanism that turns HIV into AIDS. The vampiric virus works the same way. The virus attacks multiple systems and effectively leads to a full-blown acquired syndrome in the host's body.

"Are you hopeful that Dr. Rice will be able to find a cure?" I ask. After all, the pair have highlighted how difficult their predicament is in their videos and blogs. With the limitations on them, who wouldn't want to return to "normal?"

"We're not holding our breath," Peter says. He catches

himself in this colloquialism and laughs. "Even if we were breathing." He pauses for me to appreciate the dark humor. "This is a full-body syndrome. If he can find ways to mitigate some of the worse symptoms, we'll be happy with that. Viruses aren't cured, they're treated. We know that. We don't have daydreams of a return to our old lives." Peter speaks firmly about this and Ursula reaches out for his hand. I can see this is something they would want, the longing in their eyes. But they have accepted this lot in life. I'm meeting them after they have long passed the different stages of grief, the mourning for their mortal lives. They didn't ask for this virus, but here they are: advocating for their kind.

"What about a vaccine?" I prod. Dr. Rice's latest research has focused on the origins of the vampiric strain. The virus seems to have begun millennia ago, perhaps before the common era. Perhaps even further back than that.

As we have all become armchair and social media virologists in recent years, you may be able to follow his latest work more easily than if he had published a decade ago. Rice has worked with the most senior vampires he can find to test their blood. "Getting them to agree to meet me was incredibly difficult, but I appealed to their vanity," Rice lamented in his recent book, *Blood Line: Mapping The Origins of The Vampire Germ To Foresee The Future of Coexistence.*

"Studying the blood from vampires created 500 years ago, we can see how the virus has mutated compared to those of the newer vampires. It appears that like any virus, it has evolved to survive," Rice explains in his book.

Originally, it may have been airborne, spreading through tribes and hamlets, eradicating the population and leaving the remaining vampires to starve with no blood to feed on or to continue to the next town and infect more. But the virus had to evolve to be less lethal to survive. The virus mutations and variants eventually morphed into what we commonly know today as the vampire germ. The virus must be spread through a direct intravenous fluid transfer – a bite into a major blood vessel. With a less transmissible disease, the hosts can feed and control how many companions they create. This keeps competition for warm blood low.

Dr. Rice's concern is that as new layers of permafrost and ice melt, releasing water and other captured particles, the original vampiric strain could reappear. The clock is ticking to find a vaccine for those who want to protect themselves against it. But immortality is an alluring symptom. Or at least that is what the fantasy novels sell us.

Peter acknowledges my question and the information loaded within it. He and Ursula know of Dr. Rice's work. "We all want to see an effective vaccine before any resurgence of the original strain."

There is a finality to his words. A topic closed off; time to move on. Or back.

"With the challenges of the initial infection, you didn't get to travel much then?" I steer the conversation to their initial years as vampires. I pull my jacket close around my neck; the night air has grown chilly. But my action is because I imagine the throbbing veins in my neck giving my nerves away.

"Yeah, the first year was tough," Ursula begins to detail their convalescence. They spent the first 12 months of their vampire life self-isolating and self-loathing. Then they realized they had a unique situation they could take advantage of.

"We never had to sleep. We never had to miss anything." Peter explains with excitement, as fresh as the day it dawned on him.

"But we were broke," Ursula pipes in, a story they've shared multiple times, the beats well practiced.

"It's hard to imagine seeing the country, especially given our limitations and need for anonymity, when we had no money." Peter continues as he shifts forward in his camp chair, leaning into the story. "So, we got back to work. It's easy enough to find a job where you start work before the sun is up and leave after the sun goes down without ever seeing the light of day in between. It's America, after all."

"And since we didn't need to sleep, we took up a night shift as well." Ursula continued.

"We worked different jobs during the day, but we both worked the same all-hours bar at night so we could at least see each other."

"That sounds like both a hustle and a grind," I remark.

"It was," Ursula is quick to jump in. "We would never try it again now. We did this for years and saved up quite a bit. After the first round of this, we spent it all. Slowly, on our first big trip down to Central America. But after that, we had to go back to the double shift work to be able to afford to travel again. We realized we were better off investing it."

And invest they did. Instead of keeping all their take-home pay in cash, they split it — half to funnel into their next trip and the rest to investments.

To hear Peter and Ursula tell it, this is the first true misconception about vampires propagated by popular fiction. "So many storybook and movie vampires are independently wealthy. I guess that helps with the plot;

they never have to work. Who doesn't want that fantasy? The truth is, most of us have only just been able to find honest work in the online marketplace in the past decade or so. Many are scraping by, living as animals. We have the least ability to provide for ourselves and the longest horizon to stretch our means for. We'll live forever. That's an awfully long time to fund our shelter, clothing, travel, etc." The pair are sympathetic to the indigent vampires still in hiding, offline, unable to connect with others for support.

Peter and Ursula have minimal expenses. They own their electric sprinter van that runs off their batteries and high-end solar panels on their roof. They have durable clothing from popular outfitters that offer a lifetime warranty, and their Social Security checks cover the fees they pay for camping and minor repairs to the vehicle. (Yes, Peter and Ursula are collecting Social Security. Peter is 70 and Ursula turns 68 this month even though neither has aged a day since they were changed in 1977.) Peter has also mastered the art of investing with what he calls a "forget it" strategy.

"I put the money in an index fund and then I forget about it. Every so often I'll check, and yep, there's more of it. We've let it run and don't plan to draw down on anything for a long time."

While neither discloses their full net worth, Peter says they aren't worried about running out at this point.

"We're going to be around a long time, and we've already seen inflation cut into our nest egg. But the beauty of compounding interest is that with enough time your money just keeps growing. Time is what we have." And what they do elect to spend their money on now is influence. The pair have made it clear that they intend to put their money where their mouth is regarding their political agenda.

Yes, they have an agenda. Don't we all? Except they have a captivated following and the financial means to influence political change. Or at least that is what they are hoping for.

"We've lived long enough to see the climate problem get kicked down to the next generation twice, and we as a society just keep trying to kick it down to another. We're going to live through the consequences of climate inaction. Maybe we can't undo what has been done, but we can be better stewards of the land, of the sea. We can make better use of resources. We can get our act together so that the most vulnerable in society aren't literally underwater in a few years." The fire in Peter's voice crackles along with the actual fire before us, his eyes alight with passion.

I hear the kindling pop before us; it calls all of our attention. The night is cool. I can feel the chill in my bones, but it is a blessing. No mosquitos biting even though I can hear the usual night sounds of bugs in the distance. Perhaps my company is what is keeping all the critters, big and small, away.

I want to follow Peter's opening to discuss their plans for climate action. But instead, I stick to my list of planned questions. "With all that money, where did you go?" I ask, eager to venture back to familiar territory: epic road trips and enviable experiences.

"Border-crossings are kind of tricky," Peter says as he leans back in his camp chair. His lack of direct answer is telling. Ursula lets on a bit more as we chat about their trips south of the border in the late 70s and early 80s. The pair drove their V.W. Bus all the way down to Costa Rica on the money saved up from their first round of non-stop work. They trekked through cloud forests, scaled volcanos, and swam with whale sharks. All nighttime activities they enjoyed by themselves. It was an epic adventure, but it couldn't last forever.

And they haven't been back. They spent most of the early 80s working their way north through Mexico, living off the money they had saved. When it was all gone, they knew it was time to come back home. But the bus never made it back across the border.

"The thing most people don't realize is that getting into another country is kind of easy. Getting back into the U.S. is another story." Ursula explains.

"The border agent didn't accept our passports. At that point, we were in our late thirties and our passports had not only expired, which was our fault for staying in Central America for so long. But we also looked exactly like our passport photos when we should have looked a good 15 years older." Peter recalls this encounter and his eyes seem to focus on whatever memory is swimming in his mind.

"I wonder if the bus is still in the impound lot at the Tijuana crossing?" Ursula asks with a bit of a laugh, trying to make light of this story.

Without valid passports they can't *legally* cross in and out of the United States, which doesn't mean they haven't crossed on foot. (They never specified how they got back into the U.S. in this situation.) They certainly couldn't admit it to me – a journalist - or online to their worldwide base of fans.

This is just another complication the two have to endure. Their birth certificates are valid and real, but try telling that to the Social Security Administration. When they went in to file paperwork, Peter had to show their Instagram page to the clerk for her to believe them.

"As we get older and older, the people who knew us before are getting older too. Soon no one will be alive who knew us before we were infected. They're our only evidence that we're telling the truth. Meeting with you and seeing others in person, once people see us, they can believe us. But nothing like an old friend to help confirm it too," Ursula offers a solution to the challenge of how they can validate their age.

"We realized upon our return that getting our jobs back was going to be tough. We were pushing 40 and still looked 25. It wasn't a huge stretch, but it raised a few eyebrows. We knew we would need to focus on self-employment. But it wasn't like it is today. Anyone with a smartphone can start posting, creating content, and if they know the algorithms, start making money online. In the 80s, that wasn't so easy for us. We did a lot of under-the-table work. Lots of little cantinas up and down the Pacific coast would pay good money for waiting and busing and didn't blink when we asked for cash. It helps that we are pale. We know many would have sent us packing if we had darker skin."

Ursula chimes in here. "We can't tell you how happy we were when the internet came about. It was like a whole new world opened up for us. We started learning HTML and built websites for hire. We started selling stuff on eBay. We could work anywhere and at any time."

After the second stint of round-the-clock working, the duo realized they needed a better way to earn money. One that wasn't so demanding and draining.

Through the end of the 80s and into the 90s, they spent winters in Alaska enjoying the wonders of the northern lights. They started a photo tour company, a nighttime gig, guiding tourists to the perfect spot to capture the aurora borealis. They shared tips on how to capture the lights through longer lens exposures and which settings resulted in the smoothest images.

With the dawn of the internet, they found an audience and a revenue stream. The pair began to post on a web 1.0 blog their tips and photography forecasts for which area had the best chance of catching the lights.

No one suspected a thing. Night sky images were their thing. But eventually, all influencers have to face the camera — a risky proposition for two people passing as humans in a culture that demonizes vampires.

Even with their current status as pseudo-celebrities, I can see that old habits die hard. They restrain their smiles, the two very intentional about how much tooth they expose. But a laugh from Peter reveals the long canines. A moment when Ursula is deep in her story, she lets her guard down and her gums show. The mask slips a bit, and I can see the evidence with my own eyes.

They are vampires.

And for all their talk of financial scrimping and

hustling, it is clear that they don't need money. They need blood.

I can't avoid the question. It is the one thing everyone knows about vampires: they feed on blood. So how have the pair survived for decades? Are they killers, murderers, as their critics claim?

The answer they gave was comically simple. True to their hippie roots, Peter and Ursula work with small sustainable farms up and down the Pacific Coast for their nutritional needs.

"Most butchers know that letting the animal bleed after they are slaughtered takes time, and the blood has to go somewhere. It has to be cleaned up. When we are in the area, we let these farmers know, and they give us a call when they have an animal they are about to kill. We take care of the bloody part and, well, the killing part for them. But we only work with farmers who are committed to an organic and sustainable operation." Ursula explains.

"Sure, we could feed off the CAFOs in the Midwest, but it doesn't jive with our ethics." Peter refers to the concentrated animal feeding operations where animals are kept in groups of 1,000 or more to make feeding more efficient for mass-scale farming initiatives. One of many environmental blights they call out on their blog.

The blood is necessary for their diet, but they only need to feed on a whole steer once or twice a month. Both Peter and Ursula take iron supplements. *Hyperanemia vampiraxis* is the official diagnosis, although their symptoms aren't solely caused by a severe lack of iron. Their teeth, their skin, ageless bodies, and no longer requiring sleep are inexplicable. Their extreme intolerance to sunlight is another element of the living myth.

"Have you ever tried stepping into the sun?" I ask casually.

"No, but if the roles were reversed, would you risk it? It's like me asking you if you would jump out of a plane without a parachute. Maybe you'll bounce?" Peter responds with a dare. I get it.

"And the blood donations, you don't feel guilty about that? Those liters could have gone to save lives." I inquire. The couple has instructions on their website where fans and followers can donate to their private blood bank.

Ursula corrects me. "Those donations still save lives—our lives."

I get the feeling this is just another aspect of their lives that they have agreed to partially share with me, more secrets that they can't reveal. The two assert they are law-abiding citizens. They aren't hurting anyone. But there are some questions they are too skillfully sidestepping for me to ignore. *How did they survive for all those years before this farm arrangement? Were they stealing from blood banks or obtaining the hemoglobin in a more – direct – manner?*

I sense a strain in their expressions. Can they detect my suspicions about their early years, of how they survived their initial isolation? Swallowing my fear and journalistic integrity, I don't ask the question. I let it sit there, unspoken.

Spending more time asking them about each fictional facet, what is real and what is not, is tempting. But like anyone living with chronic illness, they are more than their diagnosis. Their story is one they want to share, and their message and mission are the reason they acquiesced to this interview. I turn my focus to their new life as social media influencers.

As the new millennium dawned, the pair expanded their brand. From a basic blog to an upgraded website. A profile on now forgotten sites like DeviantArt. A Tumblr feed too, for a while. They embraced each new platform to continue sharing their park and nature photos and their life on the road. But they never shared their names, their real story. As Facebook and Instagram came on the scene, they adapted once again.

Their cache of images finding a new home for a new generation.

"So, when did you decide to 'go public'?" They had been living online for almost two decades before facing the camera. The pair only announced their vampirism to the world twelve months ago after growing their following online for years.

Their first post to Instagram in 2013 under the handle @PeterandUrsulaPics was of the Milky Way over Death Valley. Their night sky photos and day-in-the-van-life stills of posters on the wall and books in their van gave followers the escape they wanted. The image of life on the road, seeing the stars, cozying up with a good book. But they never appeared in any of the photos for years as their following grew.

Then, in 2018, they began to show themselves in the frame, but no selfies. Peter and Ursula were clever about their exposure. A hand on a coffee mug, Ursula staring out at the early night sky from the campfire next to their van, her back to the camera. Ursula usually starred in their photos.

"That's the #vanlife requirement. Pretty girl in the well-designed van with a nature view out the back window." But that was a little tricky for the pair since they were limited to the confines of their van during the day. "We can only post so many photos of the night sky before we just become an astronomy account," Ursula adds.

Just like any good social media influencer, the pair have monetization schemes outside of video views and sponsored posts. Ursula created a National Parks at Nighttime guide. The PDF contains tips on stargazing and backcountry camping that amateur photographers can purchase on their website. Peter is focusing his efforts on an app called No-V, for anyone looking to avoid the sun. It is popular among melanoma survivors.

In 2021, the duo decided it was time to address their unique posting style. Many fans and followers enjoyed the different focus on their accounts. Peter and Ursula weren't following the formula of other #vanlifers by posting impossible-to-catch sunrises and sunsets. In fact, they seemed to garner more support because they played it safe. No daring shots of yoga on a precipice. They showed real vanlife for real people. Nothing that seemed too unattainable. Or so it seemed.

On May 26, 2021, the two posted their first "usie," a photo the pair took of themselves with beaming smiles. The post to their 250,000 followers extended well beyond the reach of their audience. The photo went viral. Chances are you've seen it too.

Because, of course, when they decided to share their first photo together, it was obvious.

The eyes. The teeth. The skin.

The caption explained their life as vampires, their life in the darkness. The post was intended to be their introduction to the light, their coming out moment.

Nonbelievers claimed it was a filter, a clever augmented reality setting to change their features in real time for the camera. Just as you can take a photo with cat ears or add a beard, there are "vampire eyes" filters. But none as rich as the real thing. And none of these filters work in real life. The man and woman before me have pinkish-red eyes and stone pale skin. Having touched their hands, I can tell you that they are not made of marble or diamonds. Their skin is firm and cold, but it gives a little. It feels like rigor mortis, but they don't smell like decomposition. They smell earthy and warm.

Trolls and debunkers were quick to invalidate their confession. "Fake news" and "photoshop!" were comments echoed on the post by many. Others offered their version of internet preaching, condemning the couple.

Ursula pops in with her own criticisms of their eccentric followers. "I'm not sure which is worse: those who want us dead or the fetishists."

With the rise in vampire stories in popular culture, there are many who take it too far. They not only want to read the books and watch the movies, but they also want to be a vampire: sporting dental implants, caking on pale concealer, and wearing black clothing and chokers.

Many can't stop with playing pretend, though. "We get a dozen DMs a week asking us to 'suck their blood.' You can tell some are playing around. Some people reach out on our Patreon page and ask if we are open to payment for 'services.' Some just leave it open-ended. Others are more specific. They want this infection, this virus." Ursula sneers as she recounts this.

"Or a threesome, or orgy," Peter adds in, clearly not amused. "We didn't care for that nonsense when we lived through the seventies. We're certainly not here for it now." And then it hits me that even though the man I'm looking at by all appearances is younger than me, a Gen Z hipster with a man-bun and a thriving hoard of followers on social media, he is the same age as my grandfather.

"It didn't help that they cast the handsome A-listers in the movies," Ursula rolls her eyes. "We have learned to click delete on the gross comments and move on."

The two have been on the receiving end of a lot of attention. With it comes all kinds of kinds, as they say.

They get religious fanatics who send them crosses and garlic, "I guess they want us to die, and it is the least menacing way for them to say it." Ursula rolls her eyes.

Neither the cross nor the garlic physically affects the couple, but the threat remains. "It's like they want to say 'you should die,' but they don't have the guts to actually say it. So, they send a cross and get to pretend that they are trying to 'save us.' No, we got the message loud and clear. You thought it would kill us as soon as we opened the package, not very 'love thy neighbor' now, is it?" Peter rests a hand on Ursula's shoulder as she recounts this, calming the anger in her voice.

Peter and Ursula have taken to donating the crosses they receive. "Someone needs them. For people out there really hurting and suffering, who need a guide, who need hope, who need meaning, the Church can help them get on their feet. There are good people out there who want to help, and they happen to be Christian. The ones who go around shouting they are followers of Christ, but want to see us dead, want to see anyone who doesn't look like them or act like them dead, they aren't Christians."

No equivocating, no apologizing for their critics. Peter and Ursula seem to have transcended above this human habit. As though the vampiric virus has erased all quibbling from their thought process, their opinions fixed and clear.

One human trait they haven't been able to shake is anxiety. Ursula talks about their nerves and hesitation to reveal themselves. Their "coming out" photo was not "insta." The pair meticulously planned the post and unscheduled it several times before finally letting it go live. "We follow a lot of fantasy and fan fiction accounts for vampire stories. We saw this huge community who would be pretty stoked to know we were real. After *Twilight*, we didn't feel as nervous about people hating us on the spot. But of course, we knew there would be 'haters,'" she adds in air quotes. "There always are. It wasn't anything we hadn't heard before, but we just heard it a lot all at once," Ursula says, her expression unclear.

"But for every negative comment, we had even more supporting us." Peter reminds her. "Some of our tried-and-true followers said, 'I knew it!' Some sent us donations that day, sharing photos in our DMs as they sat with an IV in their arms. We have a great community, and that is what really shone through."

And those donations weren't to fund their lifestyle. Followers went to private blood donation centers and contributed liters and liters. Some of this blood went to Peter and Ursula directly. My thoughts flashed back to the small fridge in their van. But they also donated blood to other vampires, still in hiding. They receive the frozen coolers and drive to different camps in the evening to ensure their fellow fanged friends can survive another night.

The fire between us crackles, pulling us back to the present moment. Ours is the only campfire left. The other hikers have turned in for the evening. The park around us is completely obscured by darkness. The light from the stars above is captivating, the night sky a deep purple.

Peter and Ursula's faces glow in the orange light of our fire. They looked normal, their skin tone richer and more alive. But the shadows cast by the fire serve as a warning. These people are predators; they are at the top of the food chain. I let the silence sit for a moment, a common trick in my line of work. It is amazing what a few moments of silence can do to loosen someone's lips. Our human tendency is to fill the silence, to connect. Our social instincts just take over, and we can't stop. But Peter and Ursula are not human, at least not anymore. They don't jump to fill the emptiness.

I press the cool metal thermos to my lips only to find it is empty. The coffee is already in my system, but the caffeine is weak against the heavy black blanket of night. My eyes are dry; my limbs are aching for a bed to fall into.

As if reading my mind, or at least the disappointment on my face, Ursula offers to refill my coffee. But I decline. They would have to boil another pot, and it is far too dark out to go to all that trouble. She insists that I at least have some water.

I offer my thanks. As we wait, Peter searches my face, examining me closely. In all my years, I have never been the one under such scrutiny in an interview. "Tell me about your life," Peter begins just as Ursula pops back with a full mug of water. Using this as an opportunity to gather my thoughts and prepare a response, I take a sip. Too big a sip, I nearly cough out the excess.

"That's not really what I'm here for," I respond. "No one wants to read about my life. You're the story," I say, focusing on flattery. Something everyone is susceptible to. Almost everyone.

"But we have all night, and after all, you're the first to interview a vampire. A real one. Not a book or movie one," Peter jokes with a smile.

"Did you see the movie?" I ask, desperate to change topics.

"Twice!" Ursula squeals with delight. "We got a real kick out of it!" Her laugh tells all. To many, the story was too scary, too seductive. But to Peter and Ursula, it was an imitation that fell short of reality. A bad impression. A joke, and only they understood the punchline.

"A bunch of us went," Peter reminisces with a smile.

"So, how many more are there?" The question I've been dying to ask finally has an organic opening.

"We don't know everyone, and not everyone wants to know us," Ursula explains. The vampire community has survived because of their anonymity. With these #vanlifers turning their back on that code, they have found themselves ostracized by many. Not accepted among vampires, not welcome among humans. The two are in exile among us.

"Don't you worry the others will seek retribution for outing yourselves?" I ask.

"They haven't yet. And it would be very obvious if we suddenly stopped posting. Our followers, and sponsors, would notice quickly. And you don't go after another vampire. You just don't." There is a deep belief here, an unspoken code of ethics.

They have a few allies in their world, and their ranks are growing. The old guard of vampires are starting to be outnumbered by this newer generation. The secrecy and cloaks, the darkness and daggers of the ancient era have been called into question. Young vampires like Peter and Ursula are finding humane ways to coexist and share the planet with humans. They are embracing the human aspects of their nature instead of eschewing them.

Peter and Ursula don't give me any idea of the size of their community. They don't have to. Dr. Stefan Maier of Arizona State University studies vampires. He estimates anywhere between 1,000 to 10,000 living among us around the world. The numbers are hard to pin down as only a few have made themselves known.

Other out vampires include an L.A.-based D.J. and a few who started a cohousing network in Canada and live in a commune-style compound. The rest have kept their secret, kept hidden. But for those few brave ones to go first, they are blazing a trail for others. The tides are turning within the vampire community, and that can have implications for the rest of us.

Maier recently released their findings on what he has named "coven collapse disorder." A social anthropologist, Dr. Maier, has one question driving their research: "what happens when a vampire doesn't have anyone they are accountable to?" In a recent television interview, Maier explained the origin of his research and subsequent findings.

"When a vampire no longer has their coven, their tight-knit group, what is to stop them from killing conspicuously? What is to keep them to any code of ethics? As we began to hear more and more about vampires coming out and doing so as solitary units, the growing concern was that the isolation associated with that lifestyle would lead to an entire collapse of the vampire society. We must remember that, at their core, vampires are humans. Our species is a social one, and we need connection on a primal level." Most of what we know about kinship among vampires is that the person who infects the host is considered a master over the new vampire. "This kind of dependent relationship can turn very toxic," Maier explains.

The initial research led him and his team to the dawn of the internet, and their original hypothesis was that the vampires who abandoned their covens were finding a new network through the internet. But as their research soon identified, the availability of online connections led vampires to leave their makers, their masters, and strike out on their own. These individuals were suddenly free from the person who created them; they could find connection with other vampires, which was a very freeing moment for them.

Peter and Ursula are cited in Maier's research as they have helped foster vampires around the world. Ursula tells me about her work with new vampires. Scared and afraid and unsure of what to do next. She does video calls and counsels them.

"I couldn't find this information anywhere online," I remark as she tells me some of her advice.

"You won't," Ursula says. "There is the web and then the dark web and then there is the vampire web," she explained. A network of people like them—other vampires—now they can find each other.

Maier explains this new social network in his book *When Covens Collapse*. "The availability of foster masters online has allowed new vampires to come to terms with their new identity and disorder. Sometimes they have hard questions about their symptoms. Other times, they just want tips on what to do to pass the time. The concept of the maker being the master is starting to dissolve."

Maier cautions that this could lead some of the elder vampires to go on a rampage of creating and abandoning new vampires out of spite, but so far, that doesn't appear to be happening.

While Maier wants to help catalog and identify the true vampire population to understand the growth and demographic shifts, he is also aware that many do not want to be documented in any way. This is especially true given the recent rhetoric floating in Congress about an official vampire registration mandate.

"Speaking of not everyone wanting to know you, do you worry about the current public discourse around vampire identification?" While Peter and Ursula have a political agenda, there are plenty of others in Congress who have their own. A junior senator out of Florida and a first-term congresswoman from Georgia have put forth a bill that could create "VampCamps." Both campaigned on a Vampire Registration and Relocation plan, among other things.

"They say we are monsters, that we're murderers. Humans without the vampiric virus are murderers too. But they aren't incarcerated until they are found guilty, until *after* they've committed a crime." Ursula's passion and fire are present, the reds of her eyes widening. The proposed relocation camps are eerily familiar to the Japanese Internment Camps of the World War II Era. Another stain on a country with a long history of persecuting anyone who doesn't fit the Anglo-Saxon ideal.

"Yeah, Georgia and Florida are carrying the flag on that one," Peter sighs as he considers this scenario.

"As if any of us would *want* to be in either of those states," Ursula chimes in. But, of course, any federal legislation would apply to Peter and Ursula anywhere they are in the country. One they can't legally leave without a valid passport and visa.

"We're optimistic that any proposed legislation wouldn't get the vote." Peter's words tell me one thing, but his voice lacks confidence. "We are honest people. We don't break the law; we don't hurt people. We want to live above board, out of the shadows. We lost a lot of friends in our community when we came out. It's," he pauses, censoring himself. "We're supposed to stay anonymous. The term coven implies more than an assumed family group. It is also meant to be secret. Hidden." Peter explains. "But now we can make our coven with other vampires around the world. We connect with them online at any time. And we have a beautiful family of fellow #vanlifers (humans) who are just as environmentally minded as us." A true budding politician, Peter has turned the topic back to his cause.

"Do you worry your message will get lost in your identity?" I ask. "People only see and hear one thing when they look at you."

"Ugh, identity politics." Peter groans. "Because my very nature has now become a political statement instead of a state of being. Look, it shouldn't be a 'this side' or 'that' when it comes to our planet. We have to live here. There is no alternative. Sticking our head in the sand or rehashing the same political issues once law is set is theater, bread and circuses. And none of it gets any of us, human and vampire alike, closer to a solution for our planet."

"Does the proposed vampire legislation give you any pause about your political ambitions?" I ask.

"No." Peter and Ursula say in unison.

An owl calls out in the distance. The sound gives us all a moment to pause. I can see the couple across the fire from me are agitated. They sit with their anger for a moment. I can see the exact moment they control their emotions again. Their faces relax, and their shoulders descend. Ursula leans back in her camp chair. I hear more animal noises in the offing, the park still very much alive and awake at night.

I sip on my water, preparing to ask my next questions. Because there is still so much to cover, and the sun will be up in a few hours.

Every #vanlifer eventually has to answer the question, "what happens when you hit the end of the road? When your journey ends?" It should be a beautiful conclusion to a transformative journey. For #vanlifers and travel influencers, it is a question of identity and income. *What's next?* Peter and Ursula have already reinvented themselves many times over. Out of necessity and now out of a calling, a need for social justice.

It is a tough position to be in. To be the apex predator, the link at the very top of the food chain, but having to remain silent. To have the power and strength to best any mere mortal in a match, but knowing that their fear would only drive them to dangerous actions. Vampires like Peter and Ursula are starting to speak out more, to demand more. To refuse to live in darkness.

"Choosing to be out is hard, but remaining hidden would have been much harder," Ursula explains.

"I don't think we're asking for that much. To be seen, to be acknowledged. To have a government and policies that don't intentionally exclude us from participating in society." Ursula and Peter outline it well enough. At each phase of their journey, a new path has been barred.

If you give someone no option but to become a criminal, an outlaw, then can you hold that against them? As a society, can we answer for whether we have created the monster?

"We're in an incredibly vulnerable situation. We have been since we got this virus. But with the changing climate, we have no way to predict if the sun will be blocked or not, and more days than not, it is out. The rains just aren't coming. We're running out of places to hide, to live." Peter explains, a line from one of his popular speeches about climate change that he uses often.

The pair are no longer appeased by using their platform to show people how beautiful the world is. They are ready to confront people with how much of that beauty we are losing.

Last summer, a few months after their big reveal, the

pair posted an eerie photo. Midday in downtown San Francisco, the couple walked hand-in-hand. One of their cameras set up to capture them from behind, the image showed them standing under a deep red sky.

"You know it's getting bad when the wildfires in the summer are so intense, the smoke so thick, that we can go outside during the day. The sun is completely blocked by smoke." Peter refers to this event.

Their faces were covered by gaiters, keeping them hidden from any bit of sunlight that might pierce the smoke. But small patches of skin were out and exposed. The devastation nearby gave them the opportunity to walk freely.

"This isn't how we envisioned stepping out in the day again," the caption started.

Due to recent climate events barring entrance to National Parks and wiping out roadways, the two have purchased a permanent home. This could potentially end their #vanlife adventure and their current income source. But picking one patch of land to settle on is a gamble too. What upheaval is waiting for each of us as the climate fully shifts into its new pattern? Which homes will be under water or ash?

"We think our audience will follow us as we move to rehabbing a home, they want to see what we are doing, but we know there will be a big change and some people won't follow. It will take time to evolve our audience to come along with us."

But the change in their content is the least of their worries. They continue to speak out against all the ways in which the changing climate is affecting millions. For some, the drought is bankrupting farms, forcing them to move and find new careers. For others, they live in fear of flooding, knowing their time will be up soon.

"So many people say we can't keep passing the buck to the next generation anymore. The climate crisis is here. But we have lived through so much and will continue to do so. Long after we should have passed on, long after you do too." Ursula explains.

The thought sends a shiver down my spine. I am mortal. They are not.

"We'll live through the consequences of inaction now and a century from now. Your grandchildren will suffer in that world, and so will we." Peter adds. "People think, 'oh, you're immortal, you can't die.' I can die. There are many ways that we can die when our shelter and food supply are in danger." Peter continues, his passion and anger apparent as his fist clenches.

As farmable land shrinks, more of the sustainable farms where Peter and Ursula feed have to scale back.

This leaves them with fewer opportunities for fresh blood. They must adapt their income streams as they get boxed in to only traveling at night because there is no rain and cloud cover during the day. It's not just #vanlife vampires who are facing these choices.

Peter and Ursula are raising capital to build a climate relocation center. They have plans to purchase land and construct a sustainable cohousing community for climate refugees, of which they anticipate many.

Their vision goes beyond a future place to live for the climate insecure. They want humans and vampires to live symbiotically, farming organically, slaughtering animals humanely (if that isn't an oxymoron, then I don't know what is), and one day working to repopulate land after the waters recede. One day many centuries from now.

They'll be here for it. It will take time to come to fruition, but they have that in spades.

Peter's entire demeanor changes when he talks about their planned community. He is excited, optimistic, and impatient. "We are really passionate about this topic. You might say it is self-serving and selfish to ask people to take action to prepare for the oncoming climate crisis. Well, so what? It will serve us well, and you, and every other living being on terra firma. Who cares if it is in our selfish interest if it is also the right thing to do? We must act now!"

Ursula smiles as Peter says this and adds, "We're fighting to save a planet that we only get to see in darkness."

"But you have your critics. Secular ones," I remind them.

"Yes, we're aware." Peter rolls his eyes at this.

Even with their activism and call for people (vampires and humans) to prepare for sea level rise and better stewardship in the face of climate change, many in the eco camp have pointed at the hypocrisy of their message. Vampires live forever, which means they will always be consuming more nonrenewable resources. Period. Warren Maxwell, CEO of EarthWell, was recently quoted about his stance on the couple.

"Even the most wasteful human will eventually stop consuming. But vampires will always be pulling on resources," Maxwell said in a recent interview.

Peter and Ursula disagree. "We, and many other vampires, don't consume the way humans do. For starters, we aren't getting fast food and single-serving cups of coffee. We don't eat food and pull on those resources. We will wear these clothes until they fall off our backs. We don't strain the health care system because we don't need any services. Yes, we have connected with vampire doctors for our anemia, but we aren't contributing to an epidemic of prescription pills. We are conscientious of our use. Yes, humans will perish, but they pass their bad habits to their progeny. Their waste will continue long after they are gone. Our stewardship is ingrained in us, forever."

And there are the claims that the couple, a pair of attractive white influencers, is piggybacking off the work done by indigenous advocates. Why not use their platform to lift up the voices of these experts instead? Is it a white-savior complex or a lack of research into efforts already underway to claw back the climate crisis?

The couple received hundreds of comments on a recent blog post, calling out their lack of attribution and credit to their fellow environmentalists. Peter admits that the pair are relatively late to the game, and added that some of the most prominent advocates aren't on social media for them to tag. But that excuse feels weak in an ever-connected society.

The couple recently spoke at a digital conference for online influencers. Peter's presentation of "Embracing Your Influence: Grassroots Political Campaigns & Fundraising For Your Cause" was well attended. He has spun up a new blog and YouTube channel where he will interview and highlight those making a difference in combatting climate change. All proceeds from ads on both platforms will be donated to several climate action groups, including one that funds climate-conscious political candidates. Peter is using the decades of skills he has acquired in digital media to turn his platform into a change-making machine.

The pair are divisive. Followers either love them or hate them, embrace their message or disregard it. No one is ambivalent about the nomadic vampires.

Our evening concludes as the fire dies down. An alarm dings on Peter's phone. Sunrise is in 30 minutes.

I thank them for their candid responses, and Ursula hands me a bumper sticker from their cache.

I am filled with a sense of awe as I drive away, willing my tired eyes to stay open long enough to make it to my motel. The sun rises over the Yosemite Valley and the granite slabs surrounding me turn from cool gray to bright gold in the sunlight.

How many sunrises have I taken for granted? How many do I, do we all, have left on this planet?

Acknowledgments

If you enjoyed this story, then please read this section as well. These are the people who helped to shape this story, to make it what you see today.

First, I must thank Jason. My incredibly patient husband has been putting up with my crazy ideas for so long. He has learned how to decipher my brain. So, when he sees the first very messy draft of each story, including this one, he can point out what isn't clear, what only makes sense in my brain. He interprets my misguided commas and punctuation. He is the reason why any of my work is coherent. Thank you!

Next, I want to thank the people who helped to inspire this story. I tried to weave together several threads. Climate chaos. Social media influencers. Vanlife. Vampires. The initial inspiration from some of my favorite travel and vanlife channels, Mr. and Mrs. Adventure, Kara and Nate, and Eamon and Bec, started the idea for this story. And an off-hand comment from my husband. Suddenly I was playing with the idea that "vanlifer" sounds a lot like "vampire," and wouldn't it be interesting if there was a pair of vampires who also happened to be vanlifers? Why would they choose such a living arrangement? What would their unique challenges be?

I've read and enjoyed vampire stories. I tend to be a bit of an omnivorous reader, which is why I write without regard to genre. My understanding of vampires as complex characters came from Anne Rice and her sentimental Louis and Stephanie Meyer's band of "vegetarian" vampires. They humanized vampires in a way that made them fun to read and write.

I must thank my good friends and early readers who helped answer some of the bigger questions for me. Is this long enough or too long? What is missing that I just can't see? Without the help, encouragement, and gentle critiques of Chelsea Brett and Nora Gecan, this story would probably still be sitting on my thumb drive, gathering dust. A big thank you to Josh Overmyer and Riley Rian for their early reviews and encouragement. Without people to write for, I would easily veer into deep procrastination and not get my stories done.

And finally, thank YOU! Thank you for taking the time to read this story. I hope you enjoyed it.

Author Bio

M.K. Williams is an author and independent publisher. She left her career in sports marketing to pursue writing and publishing full-time in 2019. She has published multiple novels and non-fiction guides. In addition to publishing her own works, she has helped established companies bring their information to the masses through publishing books under their own brands. She focuses on helping aspiring authors realize their dreams. When she isn't writing, she enjoys running and reading in her spare time.

If you enjoyed this story, please consider leaving a review for Interview with a #Vanlifer. Each review helps other readers discover this book. Thank you for your support.

And you can check out other short fiction from M.K. Williams:

Escaping Avila Chase is a story about FBI Agent Trevor Hobbertson, who is having the worst week of his life. Not because a hacker he has been tracking slips through his fingers, but because his ex-girlfriend with an axe to grind is releasing a new book. Try as he might, Trevor just can't escape the feeling that she'll be airing all her grievances in her not so fictionalized tale.

Who is Avila Chase exactly? She's a femme fatale with creative license, and she is sharpening her pen just for Trevor.

In this literary short story, we get a front-row seat to Trevor's aching paranoia. Is Avila really after him or is this all in his mind? A novella that will leave you haunted; *Escaping Avila Chase* provides the reader with an uneasy feeling as Trevor revisits his memories with Avila across the city of Philadelphia. A psychological character evaluation, *Escaping Avila Chase* is a carefully constructed literary novella with a narrator you just love to hate.

This short story is rich with imagery and is a book for bookish people. Read this novella today and find out if you too can escape Avila Chase.

www.ingramcontent.com/pod-product-compliance
Lightning Source LLC
Chambersburg PA
CBHW030651190726
48286CB00008B/2763